SHIPPED

ABBY KNOX

Summary

Angelica

My 23rd birthday is coming up, so I should be excited to get my royal inheritance as the princess of Austero. Unfortunately, my father, the king, is stuck in his ways and insists on upholding old traditions that dictate that I must be arranged in marriage first. I want to stick up for myself, but I also need that money to break away and start a life of my own. It would seem that I'm trapped, until a handsome deckhand makes an offer that will surely turn the tides. But am I prepared for the ensuing maelstrom with my family?

Abel

I wouldn't have believed in love at first sight, until it happened to me. As soon as I see Princess Angelica boarding the yacht I work on, I know I need a plan to make her mine. When I learn about her predicament, I'm both horrified on her behalf, and inspired. I've got an idea, but I'll have to act fast. Maybe I'm sailing too close to the wind, but I've got one chance and I'm taking it. Batten down the hatches, royal family!

Naughty Yachties is a new series of short romance stories loosely inspired by Below Deck. If you love romance tropes, obsessed heroes, plucky heroines, high heat, and happily ever afters, then welcome aboard!

Chapter One

Abel

I'VE FOUND my calling in life. I'm going to marry a princess.

I know this as surely as I know my own breath while my crewmates and I line up in our dress whites on the aft deck.

Under the guidance of veteran Captain Joe, we are the crew of The Carpe Diem superyacht, preparing to launch the summer yachting season in the Mediterranean. The sun beats down on our heads, but we are armed with cold champagne for our first guests of the season in the tiny island nation of Austero.

Everyone around me is whispering and talking out of the sides of their mouths, but all I do is stare straight ahead because I can't take my eyes off of…her.

The princess.

"Did you see the diet requirements? Maksim is silently flipping out," murmurs Vanessa, a pale Midwesterner and

the only other American on this crew besides the captain
and myself.

She says this under her breath as our chef remains
stoic, staring straight ahead at the dock. Our Russian chef
has never worked on a luxury yacht before but is already
stubborn, opinionated, and a little scary. In other words, a
typical chef.

"Why charter a yacht? I would think a royal family has
their own vessel, with their own private chef," whispers the
second stewardess, Juno, pressing a hand to her red hair
that's wound up in a tight bun. The Australian woman is
the most experienced stew I've ever worked with besides
Vanessa. Our third stew, Star, a wide-eyed brunette from
New Zealand, says nothing. This is her first job as a third
stew, and the terror shows in her wide blue eyes despite her
practiced smile.

"The royal yacht of Austero is out for repairs. The
young princess threw a large party, and, well, it's too upset-
ting even to discuss," Elijah informs everyone. My
buttoned-up supervisor, a Bahamian who towers over
everyone, loves these white boats more than anything. I've
worked with the man before, and I once saw his eyes well
up at the sight of full sails.

"I heard that the party princess is supposed to get
married on this trip," whispers Dustin, the youngest and
greenest of the deckhands. The Canadian kid is 19, and
the scuttlebutt is he got this job because his father, a
captain on a sailing yacht, pulled strings.

I study the people approaching the gangway. In step
behind the king and queen, two young women share a
family resemblance. The older one appears to have a
husband and four young children with her. Then there's a
photographer and three middle-aged folks bringing up the
rear.

"Married to who?" I ask, transfixed on the small-but-curvy brunette heading my way. I feel as if I'm watching her underwater.

Juno murmurs, "I have no idea. Something having to do with a 23rd birthday tradition in the family. They get married on boats in a private family ceremony, then the whole country throws a big party upon their return. It's weird."

Indeed, there is a contingent of well-wishers cordoned off along the dock, reaching out to shake hands with members of the royal family. The king and queen simply wave at them. The young princess is the only family member who stops to shake hands and allow selfies.

I'm 23, and I couldn't imagine getting married—not until today.

But as Princess Angelica from Austero approaches, I can already see the rest of my life before my eyes.

"Probably that guy right behind them," Juno points out.

I squint, and I see a man who appears to be at least twenty years older than the princess, his expression tight and determined.

I don't have any psychic powers, but I try anyway. That stranger might be a nice man, but I summon the gods of the sea to push him off the dock. Not really. I don't actually want anyone to drown. But this information is making me irrational. No one is getting married to the princess this week. Not that princess, and not on my watch. Unless it's me. I would marry her right now if she asked me to. But that would be crazy.

The small children seem to love their aunt and insist on fighting over who will hold her hand.

"I have two hands, sweethearts, one for each of you," Princess Angelica chuckles. The children's mother has a tiny baby strapped to her chest, and her husband carries a squirming royal toddler in his arms, its chubby fingers reaching back as he cries for his aunt. The older princess turns and says something that makes Angelica laugh, her brown eyes crinkling adorably.

Angelica's long floral dress is gauzy, fluttering in the sea breeze. Her thick curls remind me of the painting of Venus rising from the sea. While her sister is tall and lean with a striking face, Angelica is petite. She's made entirely of soft, tempting curves. In my mind, I'm already grabbing onto those hips, gripping them tight while she rides my lap. I would never say things like that out loud, but I am falling apart on the inside.

I try not to sweat about meeting royalty. I do exactly as Vanessa, our chief steward, taught us. Greeting the queen with a slight bow of the head and taking their hands only if offered, addressing them each as "Your Majesty."

All seems to be going well, and the children are articulate and polite. I've never seen a small child look an adult right in the eye and say, "How do you do?" It's all pretty freaking cute if a bit surreal.

I've forgotten my nervousness until Angelica stands before me, and I'm instantly a bumbling mess. "Ma'am," I blurt, adding a curtsy. A curtsy? What the hell is wrong with me?

"Oops. I mean. Sorry. I meant to say, Your Highness," I say as my heart pounds outside my chest. And I curtsy again as I apologize. Angelica presses her lips together, willing herself not to laugh.

She rests her hands on my shoulders and says, "Deep breath. Now come closer, and I'll show you how we all greet each other on the street in Austero."

Inhaling slowly and exhaling, I obey the princess. My princess. I bend down slightly, but she pulls my face close to hers. Her soft lips kiss me once on the left cheek, once on the right cheek, and then on the left again.

I am a professional. This is the official greeting of her people. I have no business feeling the things I'm feeling. It doesn't matter how good she smells or how nice her glossy lips felt in those nanoseconds they brushed my cheeks. Or the electricity I felt with her hands clutching my shoulders. She is a charter guest. If I want to bask in her scent, I must do it while swabbing the deck wherever she walks. The time for fraternization is after the charter. I must fight to remember that.

And then, she's away from me. She's only stepped away a short distance to sip champagne offered by the stews, waiting for the boat's tour to begin. But the distance between us feels like the Pacific Ocean.

The last three members of the party follow up the gangplank. The first man introduces himself as Duncan Radcliffe III, and then his sister, Renee, and their butler, Edwin. While my brain is short-circuiting, trying to remember everyone's names, Renee comes in for a hug, reeking of alcohol already. She whispers in my ear, "Well, hello to you."

When I pull back from this unwelcome embrace, her heavily lined eyes survey me from head to toe, and she winks.

I look to Elijah, who tells me with a subtle glance that he'll have my back if anything gets out of hand with any drunk guests. I let out a breath.

Later, as we deckhands deliver the luggage to the guest cabins, it's evident that the other deckies saw everything. Dustin is the first to give me shit.

"First charter of the season, and already the cougars are after you. Congrats, 'lead deckhand.'" He gestures with quotation marks like he somehow resents me achieving that title.

Elijah barks at him. "How about instead of using air quotes, you use your hands to get back to work, Dustin."

Elijah recites the yachting company policy, grunting under the weight of the queen's matching Louis Vuitton as we enter the primary suite.

"Fraternizing will be grounds for instant dismissal," he reminds us.

Elijah tosses me the keys to the lazerette, the stern compartment near the swim deck, where the water toys are kept, and tells me to start prepping the jet skis.

On the way to the laz, I overhear something I'm not supposed to hear: a conversation between the king and queen.

The two of them are lounging on the sun deck when I pass. The queen: "But James, dear, don't you think Radcliffe is a little…mature for our Angelica?"

The king: "Emily, my love, we've gone over this. Radcliffe inherited all that land, which means our tiny, scrubby little beaches will be mine. What I mean is, we'll turn it into the most profitable coastline in all of the Mediterranean. For the benefit of our citizenry, of course."

The queen sighs. "The older I get, the more I want someone in this family to marry for love."

"The salt air is making you soft, Emily."

I don't know much about romance or marriage, but I'm pretty sure land deals have not been part of the equation in a few centuries.

This is bad. But what do I do? I can't let Angelica marry that guy.

I make a mental note to check my handbook of maritime law, but I'm pretty confident I'll go to prison if I steal the princess away in the middle of the night, even if it is for her own good.

I'll have to test the waters with her and see if running away with a guy who squeegees boat windows for a living is a better option.

Chapter Two

Angelica

THAT CREW MEMBER, Abel, just turned my whole perspective on men upside down.

Maybe it's because he's young and sweet and smells so good, but he's awakened something inside me.

As a rule, I don't date. I've never been alone with a boy without close supervision. I have suitors. Gentlemen who my father has screened. All of them cocky, arrogant, and boring.

Occasionally I have been on outings with friends, but there's always a chaperone. The palace insisted on someone supervising my most recent booze cruise with my friends. I wince as I recall that not even the chaperone could have prevented the damage done by some friends of friends. The party got out of control, and ultimately I was responsible for not being more conservative with the guest list. You could say it was an act of rebellion to celebrate my last days of being single.

Because in my family, you get married by 23, and you get your share of the family inheritance.

A reasonable person would tell their parents and the palace to keep the money, because who wants to get married for the sake of getting married? But for me? I need it. I want to build a free nursery school to serve the fishing village in Austero.

My parents, the king and queen, are not keen on my ideas. But why send me to university abroad if they don't want me thinking for myself?

Getting married is fine when you're in love. But I've never had romantic feelings for any of the suitors approved by my father. Least of all Radcliffe. But my opinion doesn't matter when it comes to the backwards traditions of this family.

As I pack my clothes away in my cabin, my mind drifts to how my heart skipped a beat at the first sight of that blonde man in the white uniform. Abel. A sweet name for such an earnest face that blushed when he'd clumsily curt-sied to me.

My entire being responded in a strange and exciting way. There was no mistaking the sudden flush of heat that ran through me when Abel's eyes caught mine.

Abel has the sweetest smile, with a touch of mischief. I could tell nothing about him except that he exudes goodness.

I would not let him feel embarrassed. "I don't go in for these formal, royal introductions," I'd told him, which was the truth.

Was I flirting when I showed him the "traditional greeting" of three kisses on the cheek? Yes. But I've never flirted that openly before, and I wanted to. I just went for it.

Upon closer inspection, I'd guessed a few facts about

Abel, based on my experience on yachts. He's a California surfer, judging by his accent, tanned face, sun-bleached hair, and that specific way his athletic body is sculpted. A swimmer's body.

My stomach had never felt so full of butterflies around someone.

Moments later, I'd gone from fluttery to furious.

That woman had her hands all over Abel. Maybe it was all innocent. Still, I had to fight the urge to push her into the harbor.

My sister, Isabel, lounges on my bed while the other stews unpack her things in the next suite. Me, I prefer to handle my own things.

"What's going on with you?" Isabel asks.

It's then that I notice I've been huffing and muttering to myself while hanging my dresses.

"Ugh. Renee. She's so…I don't know. Obvious."

Isabel snorts and examines her manicure. "Yep. You can tell who was raised with royal etiquette and who wasn't. Hopefully, your future sister-in-law doesn't get too drunk tonight."

Sometimes my sister's snobbery shocks even me. "That's not what I meant. Just the way she was pawing all over Abel."

"Who?" I freeze. Even with my back to Isabel, I can hear the smile in her voice. It's that tone that's full of thirst for gossip.

I clear my throat but keep on task with my clothes and luggage. I can't face her; I don't want her to see my pink cheeks. "I think that's the deckhand's name. The one she was practically begging to teach her how to ride a jet ski."

The bed creaks as Isabel sits up. "Oh! His name is Abel, is it?"

"Isabel."

She's off the bed and in my face before I can maneuver to avoid her.

Isabel gasps when she sees me blushing. "You like him!"

I scoff. "Shut up."

Isabel plonks down her champagne glass and rubs her palms together. "Drama on the high seas! I'm so excited."

"Stop it," I huff, pushing past her to unpack my shoes. I decide on a pair of cute sandals for tonight's Hawaiian-themed party and set them aside.

Isabel clucks her tongue. "I thought I saw him staring at you. That's so cute! Too bad tomorrow's your white party, and the proverbial party is all over. Abel will be so disappointed to see you get married to a weird old man. Poor thing."

I answer before I even realize the trap she's set for me. I whirl on her. "Abel and I haven't even…ugh, we just met!"

Her eyes widen, and she covers her mouth. "So you are crushing on him! I knew it! Oh my god, I love this so much! The future queen has a lover on the side."

"Isabel, I swear to god. You are such a shit-stirrer!"

She gestures wildly with her hands. "I am a mother of four. Even with night nannies, I don't get out much. Give me something to look forward to other than what's-his-name."

I squeak out the name Radcliffe and shudder. "Ugh. I know. I have to figure a way to get my trust fund out of Granny without getting married. What a weird stipulation. It's not like I'll ever actually be queen. You're next in line, with a brood of your own. And if they think I'm going to marry Radcliffe, when he's just so…"

"Boring? Rude to his butler? Laughs through his nose? Has weirdly long fingernails? Eats his tacos with a fork? Drinks extra-garlicky bloody Marys with every meal as if it is his ardent wish to morph into a smelly tomato?"

"I think we've uncovered the source of his bad breath," I say, snorting a laugh.

"Maybe you can teach him better hygiene once you're married," Isabel jokes.

"Gah! I'm going to push you overboard," I threaten.

Isabel laughed. "Go ahead; maybe they'll send that hot deckhand to save me."

"You're married!"

"And you take me too seriously." Isabel flops down to the bed again and sighs. "I don't know why Daddy is so hell-bent on that guy for a son-in-law."

I snap my empty suitcase closed and stow it in the closet. "The king is always scheming."

Sullenly, I toss the rest of my shoes into the closet and shut the door, too grumpy now to arrange everything perfectly as I usually would. I grab the champagne glass from Isabel's hand and down it.

She shakes her head at me. "You can get your own drink from one of the stews."

I glare at her. "I will. I plan to stay drunk between now and the white party. And their names are Vanessa, Juno, and Star."

Rolling her eyes and muttering about how I'm such a princess of the people, Isabel stands and follows me out of the room.

The narrow hall leads to a tight spiral staircase that ascends into the main salon. I need another champagne, stat. Isabel is on my heels. "I'm sorry for being this way, but it's all in love. I don't want you marrying Radcliffe, but I haven't seen you come up with a plan to avoid it yet. And the clock is ticking. Your white party for your 23rd birthday is tomorrow, which we know is going to end with a wedding. So excuse me if I get excited about literally any other alternative."

In the salon, Juno smiles and hands me champagne the second I enter the room. I thank her and continue moving, making my way to the side deck, narrowly avoiding a conversation with Radcliffe, Renee, and Edwin, who are lounging on the salon sofa and seem to be looking over a map of some kind. Probably deciding on development plans for his parcels of virgin coastline. I shudder. Thank god he doesn't even look up when I pass.

When the door slides shut behind us, I hiss to Isabel. "What other alternative would that be? 'Oh, sorry, Pops. I won't be marrying your weirdo old friend because I don't wanna.'"

Isabel nods and sips her second glass of champagne. "Yes. That's exactly what I mean."

I study my sister, remembering her white party. On her 23rd birthday, I'd only been 13 years old. She was lucky that she and Roger were already in love. Everything about that wedding was easy, and their marriage seems just as simple, now ten years after their wedding.

"Too bad for me, Daddy didn't pair me with someone remotely interesting."

Trouble and mischief brew behind Isabel's eyes. I look away and lean over the railing. Salty sea air fills my lungs. The harbor at Austero has faded in the distance, and I realize I didn't even get to choose my birthday location. I mutter, "I could try to give everyone the slip when we dock for a day of shopping, but I don't ."

"Alright, here's the thing, little sister. You are the interesting one. Daddy's not going to pair you with anyone worthy of you; let's accept that fact. Let's also accept that you're not going to marry Radcliffe, no matter what Daddy says, because it's a stupid tradition.

You're the rebel of the family. You break the tradition. You decide."

Yes, this is what I should do. It *is* a stupid tradition, she's right.

I should give up everything: my title, my inheritance, my trust fund, my apartment in the palace in Austero. My dogs. Everything I have is tied to my family. I don't want to humiliate or offend them. Nor do I want to draw unwanted attention to our tiny island nation with a royal scandal. My birthday party with my friends, which ended up damaging the official royal yacht, was embarrassing enough.

My parents, people, and position have given me a wonderful life. Perhaps I should be more grateful.

As I gaze over the side deck out into the water, a long shadow to my right catches my attention. I turn and see Abel and the other deckhands inflating a giant slide.

My blood heats as I catch myself staring. Abel has changed out of his dress whites and into a sky blue Dri-fit shirt that hugs every muscle from the waist up. My breath catches at the ripple of his suntanned legs, the way the breeze moves through his chin-length hair. Does he know he looks like a golden god?

What is wrong with me? He's just minding his own business, and here I am, staring at his butt.

At least I'm subtle about it, compared to some people. Speak of the devil, who should ooze into my perfect view but Renee, of all people. Oh, no. My blood starts to boil as her eyes rake over Abel's body.

He's mine to ogle, not yours, says my lizard brain.

God, I have lost my marbles.

I watch in awe as Renee pretends to stumble, nearly taking Abel down with her.

"Whoa! Are you okay, ma'am?"

Renee rights herself and giggles like a schoolgirl. My gut twists, and I feel sick watching this display. "I suppose I don't have my sea legs yet. So sorry."

"Not a problem," he says with a polite smile and a nod.

Her eyes go to the air pump and the slide. "Oh my, what is that you're pumping?"

"Uhh, a slide," says the bosun, Elijah. "It should be ready for you after lunch."

She blinks at Elijah and then turns back to Abel. Renee runs a hand up the length of his muscled arm. "Well, that's going to be very big whenever you're done pumping it. I don't know how you'll manage to put it away again once it gets wet."

I am growling inside, like a grizzly bear.

Abel is confused by this conversation; bless his heart. Behind him, Elijah rolls his eyes. The other deckhand is spluttering and working hard at trying not to howl.

Me? I am seeing red. To make matters worse, Isabel cackles behind me. "Go get her, Angelica. I'll hold your earrings."

I am a princess, I think, gritting my teeth. I was brought up better than this. I will not pop Renee in the nose over someone I barely know. She is a guest of the king and queen. I have manners. I have grace.

Most of all, I have no claim on Abel. Renee wafts away and stumbles back into the salon, where Juno is waiting with yet another glass of champagne. At what point is someone considered over-served? Maybe I should say something to my parents.

Abel watches her go, and then he notices me standing there, watching. He nods, and the slow smile that spreads across his face makes my cheeks heat. Without knowing why or where the impulse comes from, I return his smile with a slow blink. That's all. I have no words, no friendly banter. I'm too preoccupied with my problems and his.

Elijah cuts the moment off sharply by barking orders regarding the slide, and I scurry away to the aft deck. Isabel and I find her husband, Roger, lounging in the sun with the smallest baby tucked under his chin. The stew, Star, fits the other three children with life vests.

"Do we have to wear these all the time?" asks Roger Junior.

Star explains that anytime a child is on the vessel's exterior, yes, they must wear life vests.

I watch Isabel scramble across the bunny pad and nestle next to Roger and the baby. Roger hums and pulls her close under his arm without opening his eyes. I feel like a voyeur, watching this sweet little moment. My heart aches to know that kind of love.

I'm too young to be married. But I'm capable of that sort of love. I know I am.

And yet my 23rd birthday is becoming less of a celebration and more of a prison sentencing hearing. I have to watch my father make my arranged marriage a media event. And I have to watch Renee throw herself at a sweet, unsuspecting boy.

If only there were a solution that would help both of our current predicaments.

Chapter Three

Abel

Somehow, I've avoided being alone on a watercraft with Renee.

Just barely.

Since we dropped anchor halfway to Italy, most of the royal family has been buzzing around the yacht in jet skis, sunning themselves on the upper deck or taking advantage of the inflatable slide monstrosity.

The children are out for a boat ride with Elijah and Juno in the tender, and I can hear them squealing as the vessel bounces through the waves.

I'm keeping my eyes on Isabel and Roger, zipping around in figure eights in the water. Angelica chatters with her parents on the sun deck above. It takes all of my strength to keep my eyes on the people in the water, which is the number one rule.

Her voice, though. It's like cool water after a day of salt spray to the face. The coconut scent of her sunscreen teases my nose. I wish with all my might that she would come down to the swim platform for a ride on a jet ski.

Deep in my thoughts about Angelica, I don't see or hear Renee coming.

"That slide is just so big it's wearing me out! I think I'm ready for something smaller. It's the motion of the ocean that's more fun, am I right?"

My nervous smile does not reach my eyes as I think, Oh my god. Someone save me.

Renee waves her arms wildly at Roger and Isabel, urging them to bring in one of the watercraft for her to have a turn. I assume this is a presumptuous way to act with a royal, but considering how much Renee drinks and how she acts with me, it seems on-brand for her.

I am not looking forward to having this woman touch me on a jet ski, but there's no way I'm putting a drunk woman on a watercraft by herself.

"Dustin! Renee needs a ride!"

In my peripheral vision, like a gift from heaven, Angelica has appeared on the swim deck, grinning from ear to ear in a striped two-piece cut so low I can see the inside curve of each breast. And, oh god, her nipples. They are hard, and they are obvious. My cock twitches in my swim shorts at the sight of them, and I forget what I'm supposed to be doing right now.

With a curse under his breath, Dustin leaves his post at the top of the slide. We don't say no to guests unless it's a matter of safety. Hopefully, none of the guests heard him swearing; it's not a good look.

Roger and Isabel zip the jet ski over to the swim platform, and I help them on board.

"You going for a ride?" Isabel asks her sister.

"Not me. Renee and Dustin," she replies.

"Oh," Renee says, disappointed. "I was hoping that Abel could—"

Before she can get the rest of the words out, Dustin and I are wrangling Renee into a life vest.

"Hey, I don't need one of these," she slurs. "I'm an excellent swimmer."

"Safety first, dear," sneers Isabel, winking at her sister.

Finally, the woman has been wrangled into a vest and seated behind Dustin on the jet ski, who gives me a death stare.

"I guess you'll do in a pinch," she says, sliding her arms around the Englishman's waist as they jet away from the boat.

My mind goes down the roster of guests to make sure everyone is accounted for. Roger and Isabel have climbed up to the sun deck to join the king and queen. The radio chatter in my ear tells me that Radcliffe and his butler, Edwin, are in the jacuzzi, running the third stew ragged with complicated cocktail orders.

That just leaves Angelica and me alone on the swim deck.

Without thinking I might be insulting a family friend, I exhale loudly. "Thanks for the rescue. That was a close one."

Angelica laughs. "You're welcome." She sits down to dangle her legs in the water, and against my better judgment, I sit right next to her.

I shake my head. "Sorry. I shouldn't say that about a guest."

"Are you kidding me?" Angelica says with a snort. "There would be nothing left of you if you had to be alone with that woman at sea."

I shouldn't be asking personal questions, but I'm dying of curiosity. "Is her brother's personality any better?"

I want to know whether he harasses Angelica as much as Renee seems to harass everyone with a penis. This is the sort of question that could get me fired. We don't insult guests; we certainly don't talk shit about guests behind their backs to other guests.

Angelica's smile falters a little. "I barely know him. I couldn't say, other than he's not my type. All he does is pore over survey maps and scroll through social media on his phone. He must be interesting enough to someone; he seems to get lots of text messages. It is odd to me that he would be on his phone so much in the presence of my parents, but I'm never one to impose courtly behavior." Her thigh bumps into mine as our legs dangle in the water, and she doesn't pull away.

There is that slow blink and a pointed look. She appears to be sending a message with her eyes, both of us aware that her parents can hear every word we say if they decide to listen. It's tough to get any privacy on a yacht, even a superyacht, and she knows this as well as I do.

The silence in the next moment is so loud the universe is screaming at me. She wants me to say something, but what?

I've seen the romcoms, I've seen the costume dramas. This is the part of the movie where the dashing hero begs the heroine not to marry the jerk who doesn't truly love her.

But again, that would be crazy. How can I trust the universe when the universe seems to be telling me to do something that will get me fired and cause untold mayhem? How can I, a nobody from California with a high school diploma, expect to have a chance in hell with a princess? It makes no sense.

"Angelica, dear," the queen calls down, leaning over

the railing above us. "Your father and I are going to have a nap."

Angelica doesn't break eye contact with me, even for her mother. On the other hand, I don't dare ignore any primary guest. I nod, alerting Vanessa on the radio that the king and queen are headed to their cabins.

"Try to behave, sweetheart," the king says, waving as they disappear into the cabin, leaving the two of us alone.

"Do you…want a ride on the jet ski or…?"

Brushing locks of hair out of her face, Angelica smiles. She takes my breath away.

"Maybe later," she says.

Her smile dims a little, and I see she wants to talk about something. So, I wait, noticing our legs are still touching. The warmth radiating off her is charging up all my senses.

"Have you ever been told to do something just because it's the way it's always been done, Abel?"

"Not much for small talk, are you?" I ask.

Angelica shakes her head. "All I do is make appearances at public events and make small talk. So I tend to skip it when I'm with people I can tell are on my wavelength."

There's a sensation when her eyes travel over my face, like a caress. Her gaze lands on my mouth for just a second, and she blinks several times.

"My first job on a boat, the bosun had me cleaning the windows starting at the back of the boat because that's how he was taught to do it on a private yacht. I suggested that for charters, it's better to start at the front and work our way back, so paying guests don't have to watch us working while they have their breakfast. His brain short-circuited, and he told me to follow orders. Five minutes later, the primary was complaining about the view of my sweaty armpits while trying to eat his eggs Benedict."

Her smile is far too generous for such a meaningless story. "I have a feeling that doesn't compare to your situation."

"What do you know about my situation?" She quirks an eyebrow.

What's that my first captain used to say? "God loves a trier"?

Fuck my insecurities. I may not have money, smarts, or a crown, but I'm a catch, and I know it.

It all comes out in a burst of idiotic bravery. "Listen. This is a big boat, but it's also a small boat. You don't want to marry that Radcliffe guy. And I want to help you. So how about you marry me, just long enough to get you the inheritance you're entitled to. And after everything is settled and you get your inheritance, we can go to America —or wherever you want to go—and you can divorce me. No strings attached."

Angelica blinks back at me. Eyes wide, lips parted, she breathes, "What?"

"I said, fuck tradition and marry me."

Chapter Four

Angelica

Did I hear him right?

This beautiful man who barely knows me is asking me to marry him. That can't be what I heard. I'm losing my mind over the Radcliffe problem.

"Are you messing with me?" I ask. My eyes are trained hard on his face, because I have to work hard to contain the urge to let them wander over that broad, masculine chest, rippled abs, sun-kissed shoulders, and soft sun-drenched surfer hair. I would love to run my fingers through it.

"I don't like to eavesdrop, so I'm sorry about that part of it. But people flap their gums when they're drinking and on vacation, and they think the help suddenly can't hear things. But you need help, and I want to help you. I don't have any expectations."

His voice is deep and alluring as molten chocolate. A

small part of me wishes he did have some sort of expectations of me.

The swim platform rocks gently with the blue water's waves. I turn my eyes away from Abel and focus on the sea. He's not wrong. And it's not like I hadn't entertained this possible scenario.

I glance around, look over my shoulder. No one is watching; no one is listening.

I can't believe he's offering me a fake marriage for no reason other than to help me. Who does that?

"I can't pay you for this favor," I tell him. "If a money trail is ever discovered, it will ruin both of us."

Abel's spine straightens. "I wouldn't take a penny from you if you offered."

I've offended him. My stomach rolls over, and I feel terrible. "I'm sorry. I didn't mean to imply anything by it. You're too pure for this world."

A glint in his eye tells me he's not that offended. "I'm not that pure."

Before I can stop myself, I answer, "Me neither."

Heat passes between us as we share another moment of gazing into each other's eyes like a couple of besotted idiots. Fake wedding, Angelica. Fake. Not real. A marriage of convenience is still that, even if you're horny.

"This is nuts," I say, not giving him a firm answer just yet. I need a few seconds to process.

"The captain can legally marry us. He's supposed to officiate the wedding between you and that other guy. He can marry us instead," he says.

This is happening so fast.

Abel sees my hesitation.

"Maybe this was a bad idea. And it's none of my business. I shouldn't be pressuring you. It's way out of line."

Look at him. Just look at this adorable, selfless man.

He's a big kid; he can't be much older than me. And he's willing to get married and divorced to help a spoiled princess.

I close my eyes and chew on my lip, noticing my heart pounding. When I open my eyes, I will simply go with my gut.

Taking a deep breath, I peek at Abel, who is absently fidgeting with his shark tooth necklace and smiling amusedly as he watches it spin around the cord.

"I'll do it. Yes, Abel. Let's get married. Thank you so much."

Abel drops the necklace, and the tooth thumps against his sternum. He looks like a man who just won the lottery. A wide, dopey smile spreads across his face, and he rises to his feet. He puffs out his chest. "I can't believe that worked! I'm getting married!"

I want to laugh, but I bite my tongue. "What you are doing is not to be taken lightly. I am in your debt."

He reaches for my hand. "Let's go talk to the captain."

But first, I pull him to me, needing to thank him with a hug. Isn't that what one does when one agrees to this sort of thing? But when Able's warm arms close around me, this feels like more than an agreement. This is a hug of a friend, with the promise of more. I inhale the salty scent of his chest, and his damp Dri-fit shirt wets my cheek. The hug continues, long enough for his ridges and overwhelming masculinity to affect my insides. He's so big. And warm. And beautiful. And hard, all over. But judging by his huge smile and slightly confused expression, he's all soft and sweet inside—a Skittle. The man is a human Skittle. And I love Skittles.

Chapter Five

Abel

ANGELICA IS WAITING for me at the foot of the stairs after
talking with Captain Joe.

I hardly had to explain the entire situation to him. He
interrupted me by saying yes.

What is it with people suddenly saying yes to the
stupidest ideas I've ever come up with?

"What did he say?" Angelica asks, bouncing on the
balls of her feet. She looks so cute I could kiss her, which I
won't do yet, and not just because she's changed into her
dinner dress and looks so regal that I start to question what
I've just done. How dare I think of taking her in my arms,
unzipping that dress, and devouring every inch of those
curves. But that's precisely what I think of when I see her,
no matter how good I try to be. I don't want to mess it up.

Still in a daze, I tell her what happened. "He said he
knows all about that tradition in Austero and said he'd do
it tomorrow, before dinner."

Her face falls. "But why wait? Why not now?"

"He said we need at least a 24-hour waiting period, and then said some stuff about laws and marriage licenses that I did not understand."

"Seriously?" Her lips flatten into a humorless line, and I can't hold in my laughter.

"Eager beaver!" I joke.

Her jaw drops, and she slaps my shoulder, making me laugh harder. "Ouch! I didn't mean it like that. Princess Angelica has a dirty mind."

Pursing her lips, she growls and reaches for my nipple. "You're gonna get it."

I catch her hand in mind, and the next thing I know, we are wrestling and grunting: her attempting to give me a titty twist and me defending myself against the surprising strength of this petite woman.

"Can't wait for the wedding night to molest me, eh?" I tease, cackling.

She huffs and shoves one leg between mine to make me lose my footing. She's so adorable when she's messing around. The physical contact, the sounds of giggling and struggling, and the way she smells like citrus and coconut conspire to make me lose my battle against the twitching of my cock.

I realize that I'm rock hard when I have her arms constrained across her chest, her back to my torso.

"Uh," she starts. "What is that?"

"My radio," I say. "You're jamming it into my pelvis."

"Sorry," she breathes. "You can let me go."

Against all common sense, I do not let her go. Not right away.

Brushing my lips against her hair covering her ear, I murmur, "Are you going to be a good girl?"

Her body melts by one degree, and she pushes her

tush back against me. I stifle a groan. "Yes?" She says it like a question, craning her neck up to meet my gaze. Fuck me.

"If not, we can settle this in my bunk. It's right there," I say, gesturing with my chin toward the narrow hall leading to the crew cabins. It would take so little effort to disappear in there with her.

Vanessa's voice crackles over the radio, asking me to come to the galley to help with service.

They can't start service without the princess.

"I have to go," she says sadly, and I release her.

She whirls around to face me. "Just so we're clear, you do not think this is a real marriage, right? I mean, it is, but it isn't. I want to make sure you don't think we'll be sleeping together after the captain does the thing tomorrow."

I laugh unconvincingly, still painfully aware of the ache below my belt. "Oh. Totally. One hundred percent. Friends."

Angelica nods, definitely buying my reaction even though my guts have turned to liquid. "So should we shake on it, friend?"

And what's wrong with being friends? Friends are great to have.

Our hands clasp, but it doesn't feel like just any handshake. This feels like something important. An agreement. A promise. She's doing that slow blink again as she did on the deck earlier today.

"How do they make promises in Austero?" I ask.

A small smile crosses her full lips. She says, "Once again, come down to me."

I obey my fiancée because any chance she wants me closer, I want it too.

She circles her arms around my shoulders and turns

her face up to me. "In my country, we seal a promise with a kiss."

I'm about to ask if it's a chaste kiss like before. But she presses her lips to mine before I get the words out. It begins as a brush of lips. But she's warm and feels so good in my arms. And this embrace is taking much longer than what I suspect is typical for settling a contract in Austero.

She pulls away, her eyes full of mischief. I know she's messing with me, and I love it. "That's it?"

Angelica nods but then fists the front of my black dress shirt and pulls me back down. Instead of another kiss, she hisses in my ear.

"This may be a fake marriage, but if Renee puts her hands on you again, I will heave her into the drink!"

A wave of heat flashes over my body. My cock's need to be released is growing urgent by the second.

"I have no doubt you have the capacity to claim what's yours," I say.

Angelica points one perfect finger at me and bites her lip. "Watch me. And I'll see you on the bridge tomorrow, fiancé."

My bosun is calling me on the radio now. "Abel, Abel. Elijah."

"Aw shit," I grumble.

I touch the earpiece. "Go for Abel."

"Get your ass to the galley. Now."

I can't lose this job. If our marriage convinces no one, and the princess loses her fortune anyway, I'll need a good job to help her out for as long as we're married. Even if she plans on divorcing me, it's the right thing to do to support her any way I can. I'll need a good reference from Captain Joe when the summer is over to do that.

Elijah's mood is thunderous when I reach the galley. His hands clasp together as if this confrontation pains him.

Calmly but firmly, he says, "If I hear of you manhandling the princess again, I will report you to the captain."

I don't ask how he knew because I know my rank and when to shut up. I nod and tell him I understand and that it won't happen again.

Even though it definitely will, if Angelica wants that to happen.

I just won't get caught next time.

Chapter Six

Angelica

"Oh my god, you're so big, Abel," I gasp, savoring every ridge of his thick cock nudging into me until he's fully sheathed in my pussy. Seated across his lap in the captain's chair, he begins to move up and down, taking me for a ride. Heat surges through me as he comes, and I take all of it, sucking it in, my walls clasping tightly.

"Milk it," he orders. "I'm gonna put a baby in you."

My teeth bite down hard on my lip, and I moan, so swept up in the moment I don't care that we're not using protection.

A tiny child's voice interrupts us. "Are you going to marry Abel?"

My eyes fly open, and the Mediterranean sun nearly blinds me.

"What?"

My heart drops into my stomach at the question from the tiny voice. I see little Gloria, my four-year-old niece, bobbing with the gentle waves in our oversized two-person float, her life jacket making her cheeks look like a chipmunk's.

I've been dozing off and dreaming about our little wrestling match in the hallway last night, and that innocent daydream turned into…something else entirely.

I'm afraid I might have said something out loud in front of this poor child. "What makes you say that?" I ask, unable to hide the panic in my voice.

"Because he's cute. He looks like a Prince Charming. Like in Little Mermaid but different hair."

I laugh. "Well, looks can be deceiving," I say. "I've met a lot of princes, and they all look different, but very few have fascinating personalities."

Gloria is bored with this conversation soon enough and switches to the subject of ocean facts.

"Did you know that your kidneys will fail before someone rescues you if you get stranded at sea and drink saltwater?"

"Sounds horrible," I mutter, wondering if my parents will sooner shove me out to sea rather than deal with the mess I'm about to create.

Chapter Seven

Abel

IT'S HAPPENING. I'm getting married.

In four hours, I'll be a married man.

I'm smiling like a fool while I finish cleaning up the deck after lunch, when I get some stressful news, however.

"We have a problem," Star says quietly, hands wringing.

"What is it?"

"The queen has decided she wants a beach day for the children, ending with a white party onshore instead of on the boat."

I pause, doing the math in my head. In my experience, prepping food, transporting tables and chairs, loungers, and water toys take hours of setup, not to mention takedown.

"Now there's no time for a wedding," I mutter thoughtlessly.

Star cocks her head, confused. "Yeah, the wedding will

be on the beach, after the birthday party. I was told to get the wedding arch and decorations ready."

I shake my head. "Sorry. Heat exhaustion, I'm talking crazy."

"Well, if you go to the beach thing, drink plenty of water," she says, her face full of concern.

I thank her for the heads up before she rushes off to coordinate plans with Vanessa.

Abandoning my cleaning supplies, I radio the only person who can help me.

"Captain Joe," I say, swallowing hard when I enter the bridge a minute later.

"You look like you're about to vomit. Pre-wedding jitters?"

"No, sir," I say, planting my elbows on my knees. "We've got a problem. I've got a problem. The primary wants to have the white party on the beach."

The captain leans back in his chair and rubs his chin. "That's gonna keep everyone on their toes."

"Which wipes out any chance of making this wedding happen."

The captain looks at me hard. I hold my breath, starting to lose hope.

"What time was it yesterday when I had you fill out the license?"

I think back. "It was about six p.m."

The creases in the 40-year-old captain's face deepen as he rubs his palm over his chin. "What a coincidence. It's six p.m. now."

Stupidly, I argue with him. "Sir, I think if you look at the time—"

"Son? Are you listening to me?"

The captain's message finally comes across, and I feel like an idiot. "Oh! Right!"

The captain laughs and shakes his head at me, then picks up his radio. "Vanessa, Vanessa, Captain."

"Copy for Vanessa."

"Could you or someone on the interior please bring Princess Angelica up to the bridge asap? We will let her drive to the island as our little birthday present."

That is pretty unheard of. "Wait, really?"

The captain cocks his head at me and waits for me to catch up.

"Oh, right," I say, realizing that's the cover story in case anyone is paying attention. "Sorry. Guess I'm nervous."

Moments later, Angelica and I are standing together, face to face, on the bridge. It's hardly the wedding she deserves. She in her beach cover-up; me in my Dri-fit deckhand shirt and khakis. Both of us barefoot.

I don't have real rings, and there was no time to order flowers. However, I guess my brain works overtime when I'm excited and nervous because I've done something to make up for that. I've snagged some table decorations and fashioned them into a sad-but-serviceable wedding bouquet. And, with bits of rope, I spent all night braiding two small bands. I only hope they fit.

We don't have any witnesses, as the rest of the crew is scrambling to throw a beach party together at the moment.

The captain is talking, but all I can do is stare at my beautiful bride, who looks nervous. Right at the part when the captain asks if there is any reason why anyone should oppose this union, Angelica pipes up. "Wait!"

My stomach feels like lead. She's not going to go through with it. This was a terrible idea, after all.

"My sister! I can't do this without her. She'd never forgive me."

I hesitate for a second, knowing that if Elijah spots me trying to track down Isabel, I'll be roped into chores.

"Please? She's in her cabin changing for the party. I'll text her and tell her to come to the bridge for some reason."

I squeeze her delicate hand and catch her by surprise in a soft kiss to her cheek. "Be right back."

Bounding down the stairs and across the foredeck to the guest cabins, I meet her halfway.

"What's this about?" She demands. "I just got this text from Angelica asking me to come up to the bridge, and I haven't finished my hair for the party yet."

I tell her what's going on, trying to hurry her along. "I'm marrying Angelica today, and she wants you to be there," I tell her when we're out of earshot on the steps up to the bridge.

Isabel stops short of the doorway. "What did you just say?"

I show her both my palms in surrender. "I know your sister's wedding isn't supposed to go like this, and that there's supposed to be music and cherubs with diapers on and courtesans and whatever the hell goes on in a royal wedding—"

"Young man, have you ever been to any wedding, ever?"

"No. And that's not the point," I whisper loudly, growing increasingly frustrated. I calm myself down, reminding myself that I have to be nice. Isabel going to be my sister.

"Listen. I don't have time to explain. The short version is, I heard your sister is going to marry someone she doesn't even like, to get her inheritance. So I asked her first."

Isabel blinks at me, similar to how her younger sister

tends to do. Calmly, with a deadpan delivery, she says, "You think my sister is like, first come, first served?"

I don't know the proper answer to this except to say, "No, I do not think that. I was offering her a way out of a crappy situation."

Isabel squints at me and looks me up and down. "Just because you're a nice and generous person? Do you think you're a better option because you're younger and hotter? I'm all for upending tradition, but what do you want from my sister? I've heard of yacht crews going above and beyond, but I need to make sure you are on the up and up."

Better say the truth here. "Not just because I'm nice and generous. But because I'll love her for the rest of my life, starting yesterday."

The sister hums thoughtfully, then sighs. "You're probably deluded. On the other hand, I suppose I manifested all of this with my big mouth. But buckle up because this is just the beginning of your problems."

We rush upstairs. I don't have time to think about what she might mean by this being the beginning of my problems. I do wonder what makes her think I need her blessing, but I'm not about to tread on that. Not now.

Besides, I'm too excited to marry the love of my life.

Chapter Eight

Angelica

Am I really going to do this?

I cut my eyes at my sister, who stands next to Vanessa. Both of them look stressed but eager to get this finished. This isn't how I wanted my wedding to go.

I look at Abel. Is this just about me getting my inheritance from my grandmother? Yes, but also, it's about me taking a stand and having a choice.

Never in a million years do I want to hurt anybody, but then again, good and generous people get divorced all the time. I'll be fine, whatever happens. Abel will be fine, whatever happens. So will Radcliff, I suppose.

I don't know much about Abel, but I believe he's good and kind and generous. And he won't hold it against me when we divorce after the dust settles.

And yet, I ask myself the question: why not marry and divorce Radcliffe if everyone will be okay either way?

"Do you, Angelica, take this man to be your lawfully wedding husband?"

And then I get my answer. Deep inside, my belly performs a little backflip at those words. Because I want to stand up for myself, because I perhaps selfishly want my inheritance, but also, I want Abel. Do I want him forever?

I glance at Captain Joe, who looks like a proud father.

I look back at Abel, who's looking at me like a man who has no intention of ever granting me a divorce. Something inside me knows this to be true. And I don't dislike that idea.

If he's not acting? If he doesn't grant me a divorce? The worst that could happen is that I could be stuck with this beautiful man, and maybe we'll realize we are compatible.

Someone's radio crackles, and I hear Elijah's voice. "Abel, Abel. Elijah. Please come to the swim deck to help load beach party supplies."

Now. We have to do this now.

So I do the only thing there is to do.

"I do," I breathe.

Captain Joe nods and says, "You may kiss each other."

My nervousness on the verge of exploding out of me, I roll up on the balls of my feet and fist the front of his shirt, tugging Abel down to me.

This kiss is nothing. This kiss is just two friends pushing their lips together. That's it.

A bubble of heat floats down my spine. The back of my neck sweats, and I chalk all of this up to the warm summer night and the lack of breeze. Let's face it; this whole situation is not romantic at all, so the tumbling feeling in my stomach must be my anxiety over the entire charade. I'm scared of getting caught in a lie.

Abel, for his part, gives an excellent performance. The

kiss is a little more intense than what we talked about, but I go with it. What else should I do?

But when I feel that tongue? Just the tip slips out and brushes against the seam of my lips. My biological reaction is powerful. I've never been kissed like that, ever. A small part of me would love to keep going, but then my brain wakes up.

I snap away from him and gasp. "Abel!" While I'm covering my mouth in shock, I catch Isabel's wary expression.

Oh shit. I'm not going to be able to carry this off. Isabel's never going to be able to keep it a secret that I married this person only for convenience. No one will believe we've been swept up in a wild, instantaneous romance and couldn't bear not to be married immediately. A moment of clarity hits me: who would believe it?

And then, like magic, Abel saves my ass. Again.

"Sorry, baby. I got carried away in all the excitement about our wedding. I forgot you said no tongue." He scoops me up in a bear hug while everyone on the bridge laughs, claps and cheers.

In his big arms, he swings me around. Isabel's gaze connects with me, and I know what she's thinking. "I've created a monster."

Chapter Nine

Abel

ON THE BEACH, on an island off the coast of Italy, my wife
is preparing to cut into her 23rd birthday as the sun sets.
This might be the most beautiful setting for a party in the
entire world, but nothing compares to Angelica in her
simple, diaphanous bridal gown. It's surprisingly casual —
a gauzy thing falling to her ankles, with a pattern of
random, tiny white flowers. She looks like a goddess of
springtime.

My wife.

I am excited as a puppy, and I can't do a damn thing
about it but stand here and blend into the background. Just
like the royal photographer. Just like the butler.

I'm still shocked the captain went along with this. How
am I not fired? How did Isabel not blurt it out to everyone
already? How is any of this real?

Adding to the unreal feelings, everything white now
looks pinkish-orange as the sun sets on the horizon.

I never thought a white party would look cool. But the reflections, the contrast, it all works. The banquet table is spread with scattered white roses, white candles, and over-turned boxes with baubles spilling out over the table, giving the impression of a heavenly sunken treasure. The cake is a white quilted fondant with pearls and edible silver ribbons. It makes me sad that Angelica couldn't have this at our wedding.

When the birthday girl, my wife, cuts into the cake, I'm reminded of my parents' wedding photos.

And before I can stop myself, I've gone to her side, helping her cut the cake, just like my dad did with my mom: my hand on top of hers, guiding the knife in.

I hear the quiet clicking of the royal photographer's camera. Angelica looks up at me and smiles shyly. For that moment, while everyone's eyes are on us, it's just her and me. She blinks, then looks down at our hands, wearing our silly matching twine wedding bands.

The king chuckles. "Hilarious, Angelica. I didn't realize we would be entertained with a theatrical performance. Are you going to break into song as well?"

The king slurs his words, but those words tell me he's still clueless at what he sees here.

Angelica looks down again and ever so slightly nests back against me. And that's when I know everything is going to work out.

"Dear," the queen murmurs, her eyes on the twin bands of twine on our fingers. She rests a hand on the king's arm, her face going pale.

When Angelica cuts open the cake, it's a shock to the senses. Inside, there is a rainbow and a cascading surprise in the center. Skittles of every color fall out, clattering and skittering all over the white tablecloth.

I laugh. Angelica squeals in delight, and everyone else claps or gasps.

The queen comments. "What in the world?"

Isabel chuckles.

"What?" Angelica asks innocently. "You didn't expect me to go along with angel food cake, did you, mother?"

Color comes back to the queen's face as she attempts to catch up on what's going on right in front of her. "It seems," she says with slow, controlled fury, "that you enjoy making a mockery of all our customs."

I wonder what happened to the queen, who I'd just heard complaining yesterday to her husband that she wished her daughter could marry for love.

The king, still having no idea what's happening, drawls, "It's just the cake, Emily."

Angelica takes a big bite of her colorful striped cake and says to the queen, "But I didn't want angel food cake. I do not like angel food. I don't like white parties. I like color and fun and sparkles and disco balls. And, these arranged marriages are arcane and medieval. Do you not trust me to make my own choices?"

The king clears his throat. "This is all very amusing, especially after the damages done to the royal yacht during the unofficial birthday party. But enough of that. I say, where is the captain?"

Isabel cuts in, surprising everyone at the table. "Let her finish, Daddy. I suspect she's just getting warmed up."

The king sits back in his chair, looking taken aback at this interruption. The queen quietly seethes but trains her face in perfect etiquette. And I'm standing here holding a knife covered in livid red food coloring, and it feels like I've already used it to stab my in-laws in the back.

Angelica clears her throat. "I just wanted to say, I appreciate this party, the wedding planning, this trip, all of it. And all the trouble everyone went to. But for a long time now, I've wanted to make my own decisions. I want to build a nursery school. And I would like to be married on my terms."

My eyes can go nowhere else, even though I know Vanessa needs me to start hauling coolers full of leftovers to the tender, the small boat that will bring the guests and supplies back to the yacht. But I can't move. I have to keep my eyes on Angelica, ready to defend her choice.

"Wouldn't you agree, Abel?" Angelica throws the proverbial ball to me.

Without hesitation, I agree. "Absolutely. That sounds like a beautiful life to me."

I sound like a complete fool. Everyone must see right through me. I don't know what she wanted me to say, but I just said the first thing that popped into my head.

The king's dessert is untouched. "That's a pretty picture you paint. The part you left out is the responsibility on your shoulders. Young lady, you must uphold the monarchy of Austero."

Isabel rolls her eyes. "We already have a parliamentary government; you have no official power other than wheeling and dealing with your corrupt political friends."

"As next in line to the throne, you'd do well to remember where your bread is buttered!" The king blusters.

"You're right, Daddy. I am next in line," Isabel retorts, "And I'll be a bomb-ass queen. All the more reason to let Angelica do what she wants."

I can't take this arguing anymore. Everything they're discussing is moot, because Angelica is already married. I have to tell them.

"She can't marry that guy," I say, blandly but loudly

enough that everyone hears it. Each head at the table whips around to face me.

Isabel sips her wine and begins to chuckle.

Angelica's hands go to her stomach.

The king and queen are not amused.

"Oh? Is that what you think?" the queen retorts. "I'd love to hear the point of view of a simple deckhand with a high school education."

Elijah hisses quietly. He may not be clear on what's happening, but he doesn't take kindly to anyone insulting his crew outside of our own good-spirited jabs.

"She just got done telling you, but you weren't listening," I reply. "She doesn't want to marry that guy. She can't."

The queen rests one arm over the back of her chair, and she turns to the side to face me. "Oh? I can't wait to hear why?"

I'm fully aware that I'm about to sacrifice the tips for the entire crew for this charter. If this turns into a disaster, I'll somehow make it up to the crew. Even if I have to work ten charter seasons without collecting my share, it will be worth it to be truthful at this moment. "Because she's already married. To me."

Complete silence follows. It's so quiet that I can hear the waves lapping against the tender, anchored offshore. The seagulls seem to be laughing at me.

And then, phony cackling. Starting with the queen, then the king, and then Radcliffe and his companions.

"My, my. This crew has an excellent sense of humor," says the queen.

"It's not a joke." This clarification comes from Isabel.

Everyone quiets down. The king's face reddens while the queen's face looks like someone spit in her food. Radcliffe seems slightly confused but mainly bored.

As much as the crew enjoys being away from the captain for these beach parties, right now would be a good time for the man to show up and smooth things over. But he's been oddly going out of his way to avoid these guests, apart from Angelica.

Angelica stands up, her hands clasped together. "It's true. Abel and I are married. I'm sorry, Radcliffe. I can't marry you."

No one says a word at first. No one seems to know where to look.

I almost wish someone would start shouting again.

Vanessa springs into action, clearing the table of plates, her staff refilling wine glasses.

Angelica and I stare at each other amid the quiet clatter of busywork, unsure what to do now, neither of us knowing what might happen next.

Chapter Ten

Angelica

MY MOTHER LOOKS down at her untouched cake slice and
silently arranges her fork and knife to indicate she's
finished. Her lips form a tight line. She has gone from
amused and dismissive to silent.

My father is also silent, but it's hardly cold passivity.
The redness along his collar is creeping up his neck. He's
building up a head of steam.

I swallow and glance over at Radcliffe, who, to my
astonishment, appears relieved. "Well, that's that, then. I'd
love some brandy on the sun deck if anyone else is ready to
go back to the boat?" He stands and trudges across the
beach and wades right into the water without a second
thought.

Radcliffe's sister is dabbing her eyes. Over Abel? That
can't be right.

My father, always scheming, always plotting, turns to
the royal photographer. "Keep a lid on it, and report to me

first thing in the morning on how we will get ahead of the story." He says these words in a tone that is too quiet. Too calm. And frankly, I'm a little scared.

My father stands, brushes past me, and marches off toward the tender. My mother follows.

Aboard the tender, Elijah steers us away from the beach. My father wrongly assumes he's out of earshot of the rest of the crew back on the beach, and he lets me have it.

"How dare you? How dare you publicly humiliate me like that? Humiliate our family, our entire country?"

Abel, bless him, cuts in. "To be fair, it's a private beach, and everyone on our crew signs a non-disclosure agreement—"

That was the wrong thing to say. My mother lunges. "You are the last person I want to hear from!"

Elijah booms, "Sit down, your majesty!"

The king barks back, "Don't speak to my wife like that!"

Elijah is not intimidated. "If your wife falls into the sea and drowns, my manners won't mean anything."

But no one is listening to Elijah anymore. Everyone is shouting and pointing. Thank god the rest of our party remains on the beach and will be picked up on the tender's return trip: I'd hate for my nieces and nephews to see their grandparents behave this way.

Elijah finally cuts the engine. As quickly as if they'd practiced it, Abel and Elijah together open a cargo area at the bow and retrieve a handful of zip ties.

They turn and face my parents, who are still shouting and stomping their feet.

Elijah holds up the fistful of zip ties, summoning the loudest, most commanding voice I've ever heard on the seas. "Do you want to follow orders on my boat?! Or do you want the naughty straps?!"

I can tell you one thing I never expected to see: the king and queen forcibly tied to the grab rails for bad behavior. I cast my eyes back to the beach, and the royal photographer is snapping away with a telephoto lens.

Shit.

Chapter Eleven

Abel

"We don't have to sleep together," I say, too quickly.

I should be in the galley helping wash dishes, but I can hear Maksim and Juno bickering down there from the deck, and I don't feel like being in the middle of that.

Not after listening to the king and queen shout at me and call me every belittling name in the book. One name I never expected to hear thrown my way was "peasant." That one made me laugh, making the king rage at me even more. I thought the queen was going to stomp her foot through the teak.

"I thought you wanted your daughter to marry for love?" I had asked, remaining calm.

The queen had pointed at me. "I have no doubt she thinks she married for love, but there's only one explanation for this. You're a gold digger, and you thought you'd struck the motherlode when you met a single princess with her so-called problem to solve."

I am not going to lie; that hurt.

Thankfully, the captain had been alerted to the situation on the deck and had come down from the bridge.

Captain Joe has a way of smoothing things over, even with the most irrational guests.

"Your highness," was all he'd said.

"You," the queen rasped. "How could you do this?"

Captain Joe had swallowed and said, "I think you and I both know how much I detest some of the customs of your country. Call it spite, if that helps."

Everyone on the deck stopped talking. The crew looked at each other. Elijah shrugged when I'd caught his eye.

When my gaze returned to the scene at hand, I saw it. Recognition flooded the queen's face. "You," she said again.

Angelica gripped my hand. "Oh, my god."

No one else dared breathe or speak. And then, the queen had hiked up her white gown and declared she was off to bed. The king and the rest of the royal party had followed quietly.

All except Angelica.

The two of us now stand alone on the deck as the moon rises in the darkening sky.

"Oh," Angelica breathes. "Right. It's our wedding night." She lets out a little laugh.

I smile, trying to break the tension. "This is awkward. We don't have to talk about this now."

"Well, we should probably talk about it. Since the secret's out, it will be in the tabloids in the next few days. So, you'd better get ready."

I want to kiss her. I also know I shouldn't.

My heart and soul might know her, but the reality is my mind doesn't know her middle name. And I'm not sure how to pronounce her country's name.

I swallow hard, trying to tear my focus away from her mouth, her sweet scent, her bare shoulder in that toga-style dress.

Once I lost myself in her kiss, curves, and scent, I would throw everything away.

"What's on your mind, Abel?"

"If…if we're going to make this seem real, I suppose we have to sleep in the same cabin, at least," I say, shooting her a wicked smile.

She nods, fighting a grin. "I trust you, if that's what you're worried about. I don't think you would try anything."

Vehemently, I shake my head. "Oh, absolutely not. In fact, I can sleep on the floor if—"

I don't get to finish that sentence because Angelica pulls me in for a kiss. Not a wedding kiss and not an official greeting of Austero.

This kiss is with tongue and teeth, torturing the ever-present erection in my drawers. "Careful," I warn, though I don't mean it. "If you kiss me like that, I might kiss you back even harder."

"Maybe I want you to, husband," she says, her lips teasing.

I'm not a guy who growls, but I feel it bubbling up. "But I thought you just wanted to be friends."

"Tell me," she says, "Do friends ever have crushes on each other?"

Right away, I answer. "All the time."

She nods and licks her lips. "Well, I have a friend right now who I have a huge crush on, and I don't know how to tell him."

I think I get where she's going. "So, you want to be like friends with benefits? What about after the divorce? I mean, divorcees are pretty hot."

She bites her lip, the sexy, juicy lip that I irrationally feel belongs to me. Initially, this piece of braided twine on my finger meant nothing. We'd decided that from the beginning, but now? Now it's like the tiny threads somehow transmit energy under my skin. I am married. This woman is my wife.

"If that's what you want," she says.

She's hesitating. Why is she hesitating?

"I don't think either of us is ready to be married," she adds.

"Probably not," I say, willing my hand to let go of her. But it's firmly planted on her hip. I'm going to get a neck cramp from kissing her like this, but I don't care.

"You look tired."

"I don't want to go back to my cabin. I don't want to be anywhere near my family right now. Except for Isabel, but she's got her own family to enjoy at the moment."

"Stay with me, wife."

A pink hue darkens her cheek. "We're really blurring this already very blurry line. Don't you bunk with Elijah?"

"Yeah, but he's on anchor watch tonight. I get to sleep."

She nods her head. "Do you want me to sleep in Elijah's bunk, or?"

I snort. "I'm not his favorite person at the moment, so it's best if we don't touch his sleeping area."

Angelica narrows her eyes at me. "Fine. I'll bunk with you. But, we're going to sleep, Abel."

A moment later, I'm waiting patiently in the head while Angelica changes out of her dress and into one of my tee shirts. When I come out of the closet-sized bathroom, I grin at the sight of my shirt hanging to mid-thigh on her.

Angelica surveys the tiny space but does not comment

on it. I let the princess climb to the top bunk first and get herself situated before I join her.

Lying on my side, I study her profile, or what I can see of it in the dark. Her lashes blink. I want to kiss that nose and feel those lashes brush my cheek.

Angelica sighs. "You are witnessing a lot of firsts in my life."

"Such as?"

"I'd never kissed a guy romantically before."

I shouldn't be shocked, based on what I know of her.

"Oh," I say dumbly.

"And I've never flirted either."

"Who were you flirting with?"

A hand goes over her eyes. "See, I can't even do that correctly. Remember when I showed you the official greeting of Austero. I made that up because I thought you seemed nice, and I wanted to kiss those beautiful cheekbones."

A sudden wave of lust crashes over me. "That was flirting?"

She laughs. "Yes."

I join her laughter. "Well, it worked."

"How was I to tell if it worked or not? You should have flirted back."

I huff, "Once again, I'm not allowed to fraternize with guests! And I was nervous!"

More laughter. "Right. You just ask guests to marry you."

Her tone is still joking around, but I'm not kidding when I reply internally: Because as soon as I saw you, I knew I wanted you. She's not ready to hear that. She's not ready to hear how she makes me sweat and want to write a million poems. I need to tell her these things, but I know I'll get it wrong.

"Thank you," she whispers.

Angelica adjusts herself, facing me, nuzzling in close to my chest.

This position might interfere with our plans for actual sleeping. We are all arms, legs, body heat, and breath in this bunk. Yet somehow, it isn't as cramped as I thought.

With my arm around her shoulders, she nuzzles against my chest. Angelica is warm and fits perfectly in this crook of my arm. Her hair tickles my chin. The scent of orange and springtime compels me to press my nose into her mass of curls and inhale.

Softly, she chuckles. "Are you sniffing me?"

"You smell good. These quarters are tight; I have to take advantage of the good smells when they happen."

"Do I want to know the usual odors you have to suffer?"

"I can't even remember any of them because you smell so good."

"Stop."

"I won't stop. I'll go even further. I don't remember what anyone else looks like because you're so pretty."

Angelica's body stiffens. This was the wrong thing to say.

"Looks are not everything."

I pause for a moment, considering what she means. What she says is true, but there was a certain edge to her words. Something is behind it more than just a platitude.

"That's true," I say. "I meant to pay you a compliment."

Angelica sighs, and her warm breath heats me through my layer of clothing. The heat spreads everywhere, notching up my ache for her. The need to be rid of our shirts and feel her skin against mine is detrimental to having a serious conversation.

"I appreciate the words. I wish people saw what else was there."

I understand what she means now. "You want to know what else I see, Angelica?"

"No. What?"

Here we go. I'm putting it all out there. "I see someone who is kind and thoughtful and charming. Angelica snuggles closer against me, snaking her arm across my middle and resting it against my sternum. A little farther to the left, and she'll be able to feel my thundering heartbeat.

"Some call that interesting and fun side of me a lack of royal decorum."

I scoff. "Fuck decorum."

"That will be my first royal decree when we ascend to the throne, after a series of unfortunate events that I sincerely hope never happen to my sister," she says.

"We? You forget the part where we get divorced as soon as your inheritance comes through."

She's silent for a few seconds. I hear her breathing, feel her chest rise and fall against my side.

"Yes. That. I keep forgetting that part."

Careful, Abel.

"I'll have to set a reminder once the charter is over. Or else I'll forget to divorce you," I half-joke.

She offers, "Because I'm so forgettable?"

I growl. "Because being married to you is easy. It feels like I made the right decision for once."

"Oh."

Did I say too much? Not enough? Did I come off as shallow or too deep?

I wait a little bit longer for her to respond. Or bolt. Or panic. Anything.

After a time, I feel something wet on my chest. Then, I hear the sniffle. I cup her face.

"Angelica? Oh my god. I'm sorry. I didn't mean to upset you."

She cuts me off with a fevered kiss that shakes me to my core. I was not expecting that. She slides her tongue into my mouth, and my heart hammers.

"Whoa," I breathe when she pulls away from the kiss.

"I take it as a huge compliment that you assume being married to me is easy."

I shrug, which causes her head to bob, and she takes the opportunity to snuggle in closer. Now, her hand is right over my heart. She must feel it, the way it pounds for her.

"I'm glad you can take a compliment from me," I say. "Because you deserve all of them."

She puffs out a breath, another surge of heat flooding me with the contact against my chest. "You're making it very difficult for me to follow through with the divorce," she sighs.

Good. That's the plan.

I'm suddenly struck with a fit of giggles. It starts as a chuckle, then bubbles up into a snort.

"This is the craziest thing I've ever done," I say.

"Me too," she says, joining me. "Did you see Radcliffe's face? He looked relieved."

"I didn't see his face; I was waiting for your father to deck me."

She cackles. "The king wouldn't do that to you. Not in front of a photographer."

We both laugh so loudly that eventually, there is a knocking on the bulkhead.

"Oops!" Angelica gasps and covers her mouth. "We're being loud."

I whisper, "I share a wall with Maksim. He's cool, but I have a feeling he could murder me with a look if he decided to."

She whispers more softly, "We'll have to be quiet then." A supple softness drags up my bare leg—the inside of her thigh.

I groan.

Angelica sighs audibly and keeps dragging that thigh upward until her leg rests on my navel. And the warm center of her is open and pressing against my pelvis.

All it would take is one slight movement.

I angle my head and return the kiss from earlier, capturing her bottom lip between both of mine. I lick her there, drawing out a sigh from her.

"So, so quiet," I whisper almost inaudibly. I feel a nearly undetectable movement from her, but it's there. Her instinct tells her to grind her pussy against me, but she's holding back.

And then, she's on top of me with one adjustment from me. Angelica gasps, and we kiss again until we lose our breath.

Everything around us fades. We're not in a tight bunk the size of a tin can. We are floating on clear blue water, endless skies, our skin soaking up each other. She is the sun on my skin, the breath in my lungs. Angelica is fun and mischief and adventure. We don't have to go anywhere; we don't have to have a big bed. She can have fun anywhere, making her the perfect match for me.

With her arms caged around my head on the pillow, I reach around her waist and pull her closer. Her damp pussy pushes against my hardened cock. She's so warm and wet, the fire inside me might burst out of my skin.

My hands travel up and down her back, toying with the edge of my tee shirt she wears. She softly moans into my mouth, and I drink it in; I can't have her making a single sound that anyone can hear outside of this cabin.

I lick the inside of her mouth, and she deepens the kiss.

We are all tangling tongues and clacking teeth and stifled moans.

"Abel," she says breathlessly.

"Angelica. Is this okay?" I ask this as my hands flatten against the skin of her lower back, under the waistband of her cotton underwear.

"Yes," she says, kissing my chin, jawline, and neck. She's a woman who could spoil me to death with her kisses, her fingers playing in my hair. All I want is to flip her over and rut into her. Claim her with my cock, leave my mark, leave my seed inside her. But that's crazy. That's down the road, sometime. Not today.

"I want to touch you, Angelica," I breathe. "I want to make you forget all the unpleasantness of today and make you feel good."

"Please, Abel."

Her pelvis grinds against me, and I give in to the urge to push back.

"Have you ever made yourself come, princess?"

"No," she whispers. "I've never even felt the need until…"

"Until what?"

"Until I saw you looking at me," she says.

We both pause to absorb this information, her body trembling.

I plant a calming kiss on her mouth as my hands roam everywhere. I want to touch every inch of her, hold her while I make her come. I want to share everything in the little time we have.

After I help her off with her undies, I roll her over to her side. Cradling her in the crook of my arm again, I take full advantage of the access she's granted me to her naked skin.

My hand drags down between her legs and cups her

pussy, where I find it is warmer and wetter than I had imagined.

I bite back a growl as my fingers find their way between her slick folds. She gasps at the contact.

"You say the word, and I stop," I murmur.

Her sweet face nods against my cheek as she breathes, "I will." She dabs my top lip with hers, then my bottom lip. Playful kisses that drive me deeper into my all-consuming need to be inside her.

On the other hand, I would be happy to kiss her all night and live out the rest of my life being horny for her. That would be fine, too.

Her luscious, wet pussy drenches me the longer we kiss and lick and moan into each other's mouths. My flingers explore, finding her cunt so tight, even for one finger. She's clenching.

"Relax and let go if you want me to make you come, sweetheart."

She opens up to me, and I slip my finger inside. Angelica's body twitches.

"Good?"

"Yummy," she whispers into my ear, licking my lobe and up the shell, ending with a nibble. Heat explodes through every nerve in my body.

I sink in a second finger, and my thumb finds her taut clit.

"Oh my god," she rasps as I trace circles around it. "That feels so good, Abel."

My fingers stretching her muscles, my thumb teasing, she comes quickly. Angelica lets out a squeak, and she trembles violently against me.

I hold her close and continue stroking until the shaking ceases. "Abel. Oh my god."

"Such a lovely pussy. So good of you to come for me."

Her breathing is ragged. Her hands travel all over my chest. "That was … I've never done that before. I didn't know. I mean, I read things. I've watched things. I just didn't know it felt as good as they say."

I growl into her mouth, kissing and tonguing and trying to push past the urgency of my cock. I can't take her like this. I'm not going to fuck her like this.

Angelica's hand travels to my cock, and my body quakes at the feel of it. "Shit," I exclaim, fighting the urge to thrust into her hand.

"Not good?" Angelica asks.

A laugh escapes me. "Sweetheart, that feels so good. So, so good. I just didn't expect you to—"

"Abel, I can feel you holding back. Don't you need to, you know, have some relief?"

I laugh again. "Don't worry about it. I'm not about to make a mess on a princess."

She pauses, thinking it over, still rubbing her hand over my cock, over my boxers. I grunt and push against her touch, gaining a microscopic amount of relief. Angelica whispers in my ear. "What if I want you to get me dirty?"

Her soft giggle that follows this nearly sends me into orbit.

"Sweetheart," I whisper, my hips thrusting, her hand stroking. Against my better judgment, I tell her to do what she wants to do. "God, yes. Take it. Take it in your hand, yes. Please," I grit out.

Angelica makes me drunk with need as her hand slides down the front of my boxers, and I help her tug them down my thighs. She takes my dick in her hand and squeezes. Fuck me; her soft touch might destroy me.

"Teach me how to do this, Abel."

I kiss her fervently for being so sweet to me, then

answer, "there's a bottle of lotion in the bathroom I use to get it wet; I'll be right back."

"I'm still wet. Use me instead," she says, clutching my shoulder with her free hand. "Is that a thing?"

I'm shocked at this brazenness, and I love it.

Once again, her leg wraps around me. Her arms pull me closer, and before I know it, my dick nestles against her slickness. "Fuck," I whisper. "Oh my god."

This is too close, dangerously close, to a thing that could get her pregnant.

But fuck me, it feels so fucking good.

I open my mouth, but gibberish falls out.

Angelica whispers, "Good?"

She wets my cock with her juice and continues stroking while I answer in only hums. I've been rigid since the first moment I saw her on the dock, and I've stayed hard for days. I'm so desperate for it, and I come so hard that I hit my head on the ceiling.

"Fuck!"

"Are you okay?"

With a groan and a hiss, my head plops back to the pillow.

"Yeah. Oh, shit," I rasp as I come and come, nutting everywhere, barely noticing what's happening.

When my orgasm blackout recedes, I mumble something about grabbing my phone, so she can find her way to the bathroom to wash up.

"No problem," she whispers with a smile. "I made you come in my undies. Is that okay?"

I tremble in surprised laughter. "Nutting in a pair of undies belonging to a princess? It's only at the top of my ultimate fucking fantasies."

Chapter Twelve

Angelica

I'VE SURPRISED MYSELF, but I guess I'm doing everything right. I thought I'd be a clod, but Abel is so kind, playful, gentle, and polite.

Whenever I read steamy romance novels, the heroine tends to fall asleep in her lover's arms right after a mind-altering orgasm.

I feel quite the opposite. I feel energized.

"Do you need to sleep?" I ask Abel.

He snuggles me in close and kisses the top of my head. "I don't think I could sleep if I tried."

"Me either," I say.

I love how he kisses my head. I love how it feels to lie on his chest and how his arms feel around me. I love that he's still wide awake after this little moment. I feel happy and content, knowing how well we fit together.

Then, reality hits, and a wave of sadness crashes into me. Abel senses it without me saying a word.

"Hey. What's wrong, Angelica?"

"Nothing."

"Your whole body stiffened like someone said something shitty to you."

I can't tell him the truth, can I? That maybe I don't want to get a divorce?

That's just the happy hormones talking.

Well, maybe I can share a little bit of the truth. "I was just thinking about what you said earlier. About making the unpleasantness of today disappear. For the record, none of it was unpleasant. All my life, I assumed my wedding day would be dreadful. But it was sweet. It was private, lovely, and perfect. And when I told my family the truth, you were there with me, and it felt like you were in my corner. So, none of it was truly unpleasant."

If I hugged him as much as I want to right now, I might smother him.

"If you are trying to keep me from getting attached to you, it's not working," he says, smoothing my hair away from my face. My body shifts and I try to lighten the moment. "Honestly, I don't know if I could ever duplicate what you just did to my body by simply masturbating. I mean, once we're divorced, and I'm all alone again."

Somehow, I can feel him smiling in the dark.

"Sure you can," he says, with an edge of wickedness in his voice.

My body thrills at the wonder of what he could be implying.

I take the bait.

"I don't believe you."

"You should trust me. I do have more experience."

"Prick," I joke, snorting. "Fine. Show me."

At that, Abel goes eerily still. "Are you serious?"

"Yes."

He hums like he's considering which delicious dessert he should choose. He sighs, satisfied with his choice. "Alright, sweetheart. Climb aboard, facing the ceiling. I'll help you practice, so you know what to do when I'm gone."

My jaw drops at his swagger, but only for a second. I have no time to waste being shocked at this confidence. I scramble onto his body like I'm getting cozy on a mattress, and my view is only the black night and the ceiling above me.

From this position, I can feel his chest rise and fall as he breathes, and his heart thuds against my backbone. Next, he whispers, his lips at my ear.

"You feel so good on top of me; I might fall asleep after all."

I teasingly, gently elbow him in the ribs, and he laughs softly.

He uses this opportunity to take my right hand in his. "Now, relax your body," he tells me. "Think about something that turns you on."

I breathe, "You just did that. Should I think about that?"

"What makes you horny in a fantasy kind of way?"

"Like a celebrity? Do you really want to know that? It won't, like, offend your masculinity or something?"

He chuckles. "Even if I were your forever husband, it wouldn't bother me, and anyone who you marry shouldn't be bothered by your fantasies, either."

I exhale and let the words caress me. With Abel in my ear, I can't possibly think about any celebrity that gets me excited.

"Okay," I lie, and name a World Cup champion football player.

"I don't know him."

"All the better for you then, because I had a dream about him, and he did terrible things to me."

Abel growls in my ear, and the sensation reverberates all through me. He can't possibly be jealous, can he?

The hand that holds mine plunges between my legs, pushing my fingers into my folds, and my body lights up like I didn't think possible after what we just did.

"Terrible things like that?" Abel rasps.

I shiver, and then without warning, his left hand takes mine, and he brings my fingers up and back. The feel of his lips, tongue, and teeth against my fingertips overwhelms my senses. Simultaneously, he works my right-hand fingers through my folds, finding my clit and teasing it.

The dual sensations are more than I am built to handle.

He pops my fingers out of his mouth with an obscene slurping sound. "Terrible things like that?"

My god, he sounds so strange. Is it anger? Jealousy? Like a wild beast free of his cage.

"Oh god, oh god, oh god, Abel!" I'm close to coming for a second time. How is he doing this to me?

Our joined hands work over my clit in circles until I'm coming apart in his arms again.

"Fuck!" I squeak. It's a word I don't think I've ever used before.

A soft, wicked laugh escapes Abel. "Did what's-his-name footballer make you say dirty words to yourself, Angelica?"

His hot breath and wild gritted tone aren't just making me come but pulling something else from me. Unleashing a new thing.

More. He's made me so wet I can feel it dripping, and it's still coming.

And then, he takes that hand that just wrecked my pussy and licks my fingers clean.

"Holy shit," I say, shocked at how my voice trembles.

"That? That terrible thing?"

Should I appease his ego? "No," I say. "He never did anything close to that."

It's all a lie, of course. I could not care less about that celebrity athlete. I've never had a wet dream about that man, or any other celebrity for that matter.

Even in the innocently sexy dreams that sometimes wake me up at night, I've never dreamed anyone would do the sorts of things that Abel has just done.

I love my fingers in his mouth. I love the way he touches me. I love the way he makes me pleasure myself.

Here's the truth: The next time I touch myself, I'll be thinking of Abel.

Chapter Thirteen

Abel

To say that the atmosphere on the bridge the following day is awkward would be an understatement.

Captain Joe rubs his chin. "I find myself in an extraordinary predicament. The crew is not allowed to mingle with guests, yet I facilitated all this drama. So, I want to remind everyone this is not normal.

"And I feel that I owe you all an explanation as to why I did that. I'm deeply familiar with the silly traditions of Austero, and I felt like…well, I felt like sticking it to the king. When I was a young greenhorn back in the '90s, the boat I worked on hosted another royal family. There was a princess there, and her name was Emily. I was a stupid 17-year-old kid who flouted the rules, and there was a moment when I thought I had a shot. Little did I know, that trip was Emily's 23rd birthday and her wedding day. And I was simply one last secret fling. And now you know the rest of the story."

No one makes a sound. No one, except for young Star, who sighs and clutches her chest in sorrow at this tale.

Captain Joe continues, "The family is meeting privately in the main salon. Tread lightly. Just do your jobs as if nothing happened. If my actions affect your tips, my salary will make up the difference."

I have to protest. "Captain, that's not necessary."

"Yes, it is," Juno says. I look around the room, and I see several others' heads nod slowly in agreement with her. I glance at Vanessa, who seems a little nauseous and distracted.

How selfish I've been.

"I mean, it should come from me. I started this mess," I say.

The captain scoffs. "I could have said no to you. I am your boss's boss."

Finally, Elijah speaks up. "That leaves me wondering, Abel. Will you be quitting after this charter to go away with your new bride, and am I going to be left without a lead deckhand?"

Dustin cuts in, "I'm happy to be lead deckhand. It'll be easier to find someone green to fill my previous position."

But Elijah surprises us all by putting Dustin in his place. He points at him. "You have been doing nothing but spying on your fellow crewmates and reporting people for bad behavior. That is not your job."

The plan from the beginning has been to make this woman fall in love with me. That's my job now.

"She's my wife," I tell them. "One way or another, we're going to be together. Sorry, everyone."

Chapter Fourteen

Angelica

My father and mother are dressed up for royal business. I guess this is a working breakfast, and I get the feeling this family vacation ends as soon as we dock today, back home in Austero, to be greeted by a crowd of well-wishers.

The king and queen are all smiles, and I don't know if this is a good thing or a bad thing.

"Under the circumstances, Radcliffe, the palace has communicated with some interested resort developers, and they are prepared to make you an offer. Cash. Today. It's the best I can do. Under the law, I cannot engage in these dealings directly, but the partnership between our two families would have made such transactions much smoother. I can put you in contact with the developers as soon as possible, and from what I understand, their offers are far above market value for the coastal properties you own in Austero."

Radcliffe is again looking bored. I have yet to figure out

what the hell is his deal. He never seemed interested in me —which was fine by me—but now he's barely listening to a word my father is saying.

Despite being somewhat ignored, my father turns to the photographer. "Tell the publicist that in addition to the wedding announcement, to put together a media package about the new resort. We need to distract everyone from the fact that our new son-in-law is a nobody from America…"

I cut in. "Hey. That's rude. He's a lovely person."

My mother blinks at me. "Tell me, what's his last name, dear?"

I open my mouth, pretty sure I remember what his last name is, when Radcliffe finally speaks.

"Everyone? It's fine. Really."

All heads turn to Radcliffe, who is now speaking to me. "I never wanted to marry you, dear."

I hold my breath. I'm not surprised at the fact of this, just surprised to hear Radcliffe say it in front of my father.

He continues. "I never wanted a partnership with the king. To tell you the truth, I don't want him wresting control of the coastline of Austero. I have plans to keep it a protected sanctuary. If your father gets his hands on it? Goodbye, Rhodophyta."

Is he having a stroke? "Rhodo, what?" I ask.

Radcliffe folds his hands over his untouched breakfast, and his expression is professorial. "Rhodophyta. It's a rare type of red seaweed that grows on the rocks along my strip of land. It's also highly nutritious. I intend to protect it for the benefit of animals and limited foraging."

My father, it turns out, is far more upset over this news about seaweed than he is about my wedding.

"What in god's name are you talking about?" the king thunders.

And this is where I take my leave. Not that I don't have an interest in hearing how Radcliffe is going to solve the hunger problem on Austero but because I have to tell Abel everything immediately.

Because I realize, that's what you do when you have a best friend. You want to share everything with them as soon as possible.

"Why did you even come on this trip?" I hear my father shout as I slip away down the side deck.

"Eh, free vacation with my girlfriend."

I freeze. What?

"Girlfriend!"

"And boyfriend."

"Explain yourself!"

I'm sorry," Radcliffe says. "I was quite naughty about that. When invited, the three of us couldn't resist a bit of a romp on a boat with the royal family. And also, this."

As Radcliffe utters that last word, clouds blot out the sun quite suddenly. When I look out to the water, however, I see that it's not clouds but an enormous white canvas covering the entire starboard side of the vessel.

"What on earth…" my mother splutters.

Chaos and confusion erupt as my parents and Elijah scramble to figure out who decided to hang a canvas from the upper deck.

Elijah's first act is to radio Dustin, assuming he's on some cleaning crusade that should have waited until the guests had gone.

But when I run to the bow and look up to the sky deck, I see what's happening.

Edwin and Renee have unfurled a giant canvas banner just as the The Carpe Diem is making her approach into the harbor of Austero.

"Save Our Beaches from Corrupt Kings."

My eyes widen, and I cover my mouth. At that moment, I feel a warm brick wall behind me, and Abel's arms slip around my waist. In the chaos and the shouting of my parents, they have forgotten all about their son-in-law problem.

I am still piecing everything together. Renee's not his sister but his girlfriend. The butler is not his butler. That's a cover story because they're… a throuple. And they strung the king along to use the trip to make a statement about their little environmental crusade.

He had no intention of marrying me at all. Not because he didn't like me but because he had other plans.

Suddenly, I realize that Radcliffe is a lot more interesting than I initially thought. Garlicky bloody Marys or no.

I must ask him: hasn't he noticed Renee flirting with everyone on this trip?

"She's a terrible flirt when she's drunk. But it's all in good fun," he replies with a shrug.

Abel has stayed close to me, ignoring Elijah's and the captain's shouts for all hands on deck to assist in the removal of this giant floating protest sign.

I turn toward him.

"What happens now?" I ask.

"After you've gotten your inheritance, you're free," Abel says, with a rueful twist of his lip.

"No, Abel," I push. "What's going to happen to us?"

The twist of his lips shifts into a mischievous smirk.

"Well, there ain't gonna be any divorce, I'll tell you that," he says, puffing out his chest.

I nod my head. "Oh yes, there will be."

Abel's brows come together in confusion, and I feel bad for letting him think for a second that I would ever let him go.

I jerk my head to the scene playing out on the starboard side, where the king and queen are making everything worse. Worst of all, the gathering of royal supporters on the dock at Austero is witnessing this royal meltdown by the king and queen.

And me? I'm over the sham of traditions. I'm done feeling obligated to do royal duties. I'm disgusted to know that my father only wanted to trade me to get his hands on a piece of land.

"I meant from them. I don't want anything to do with my family other than my sister. And no one will ever call my husband a peasant, ever again."

The strength and swiftness with which Abel scoops me up in his two arms are truly breathtaking. The kiss, which can now be seen from shore, provokes cheeks from the crowd.

All my fellow citizens understand is I'm married, and that's good enough for them.

Chapter Fifteen

Abel

My wife's curvy frame looks like a sculpture as she stands with her back to me, gazing out onto the sea through our room's arched stone balcony window.

The two of us have booked a small villa, far away from the palace, until we can sort out a place to stay permanently. It's quaint, but the bed is enormous and comfortable.

"I'm not taking the inheritance from my grandmother, Abel," she says, still facing away and enjoying the view from the open window.

I don't care about the money either way, but I'm curious. "Go on."

She takes a deep breath. "I'm a hypocrite. This whole thing was me trying to subvert my family so I could be on my own. And you were the easy answer to all of that."

I take a tentative step toward her. "I'm glad you thought I was an easy answer," I say, half-joking.

Her shoulders sag. I still don't know my wife well, but I know that posture. She's starting to regret all the drama we've caused. I hate that she's feeling this way.

"I'm sorry you got dragged into all this. You could have just gone on with your single, happy life. I should have said no, and let you," Angelica says.

This can't be happening. I won't let it go this way.

"Angelica." I take another step forward. "I don't care about the money. I care about spending every minute with you. Whether that means in a palace or a hovel. I don't care. Did you hear me when I said we weren't getting divorced?"

Her lips part. "Did you hear the part where you didn't need to do any of this? That I'm a sham and a liar?"

I can't take it anymore. I won't let Angelica run herself down. "Stop being ridiculous and listen to me. I married you because I fell in love with you. That's it! I didn't care about the plan. The only plan was to have you for myself. I didn't think any further than that, and I would do it again."

Her eyes study me like I'm unhinged. "You don't know you love me. You don't even know my middle name."

"It's Marie. I saw it on the marriage license we signed, remember? You're Angelica Marie Montebello."

Her throat bobs. "Abel Jacob Oaks, I love you too."

Good," I huff, petting her smooth shoulders.

"What do we do now?"

I reply, "We figure it out together. Whatever you want. I could support you, working with my hands. I can do anything."

"No," she breathes. "I mean right now. I just told you I loved you, and you said it to me. We should commemorate the moment or something."

"Oh," I reply. "Do you want to have a celebratory

dinner? Drinks? Cake? Like, a real wedding cake? We could go ring shopping! Dress shopping? Do you want to start over and plan a real wedding at the palace? Or here? In the villa would be nice. Anything. What do you want?"

The verbal tsunami that comes out of me makes her laugh, which makes me happy. I'm a simple, happy, excited puppy.

Angelica cups my face. "No, Abel. I think what we do is, you rail me in that bed until I forget my own name."

I'd planned on that anyway. But I would do any of those things I'd listed, too. That we're on the same page now confirms that I chose the right person for me. I'm just lucky that she chose me.

We tumble into the bed together, and she shrieks in delight when I flip the hem of her dress up and bury my face between her warm, damp thighs.

The sea breeze blows through our open balcony window, caressing my bare back as I feast.

I barely know her, but my soul knows her.

I plan on drinking her in, feasting on her, talking to her, connecting with her every day for the rest of our lives. It might not always be smooth sailing, but that's life.

And I might be a nobody from America, married to a princess, but I belong here. Between her legs, by her side, any way she wants me.

I belong wherever Angelica is, and I'll swab her decks anywhere, anytime.

Epilogue

One year later

Abel

THE PEOPLE of Austero are good and hospitable, and they have welcomed me into their country better than the actual royals.

Isabel and Roger and their little family have been great. My mom-and dad-in-law? Let's just say it's complicated. The king would love nothing more than to salvage his image in the eyes of the media with a heartwarming reunion with the "people's princess."

These reunions have been repeatedly called off because her parents insist on bringing their photographer everywhere with them.

"If they want to talk, we can do it privately, away from cameras and away from photographers," Angelica has declared.

Someday we will patch things up. I will support my wife in whatever decision makes.

In the meantime, Radcliffe is the subject of more positive press than the palace, with him and his partners successfully creating their little sanctuary on the coast.

On our fifth anniversary, I pick up my wife from her job at the nursery school she built for the fishing village with her inheritance. I work at the marina, and I have loved providing for her while she has been busy with her school.

Today, my boss at the marina has let me off early, with a special gift for the two of us.

"What a lovely surprise," she exclaims, climbing aboard the golf cart with me, kissing me firmly on the mouth. Somewhere around us, camera shutters click, but we ignore it.

Our life is so dull; I can't imagine why anyone cares to make a spectacle of it.

"I have more surprises if you're not too tired," I say.

Angelica threads her fingers through mine, and her other arm curls around my bicep, her face snuggling against my shoulder. I love how handsy she gets after a long day of work.

"As long as my feet are elevated, I'm down for whatever," she says.

I gun the engine and steer us back to the marina, where a small pleasure yacht awaits us. I don't answer any of my surprised wife's questions as I remove the stern lines and begin to steer us out of the harbor. Not until I seat my wife on my lap in the captain's chair do I entertain her queries.

"Where's the captain of this boat?"

I wink. "You're looking at him."

"What?"

I unfold a slip of paper that I've stashed in my pocket and show it to her. "You got your captain's license?"

Her eyes are wide, and she jumps up in delight.

I nod, laughing at her excitement.

"I'm so proud of you!"

She hugs me and plants another sweet, firm kiss against my lips. More kisses like that, and I won't be waiting until we're below deck before I bury myself into her.

As we head out to sea into the setting sun, I hear her open the mini-fridge in the small cabin down below.

"You have enough food down here to feed the entire navy of Austero."

I call down, "You're going to need your strength."

I hear her feet padding up the steps to the deck as I thrust the engine.

She cocks her head. "Strength for what?"

"For the baby-making."

Angelica laughs as I pull her to me, claiming her mouth with a deep kiss.

She answers with a sensuous swipe of her tongue into my mouth.

Growling, I know I have to stop making out with my wife, and drive this boat to our private spot.

After we're securely anchored, I return to the wheel and see my wife's face reflecting the gold and pink sunset.

"You make me wish I could paint."

Angelica blinks at me. "Use what you got and paint a baby in me, deckhand."

"Dirty little princess," I rasp, slamming her into my arms and devouring her mouth with a kiss.

"*Your* dirty princess," she replies, fisting my shirt while we taste and maul each other.

I pull away from the kiss just long enough to hitch up the hem of her dress as she lifts her arms over her head.

The kissing resumes with the grappling of hands on hooks, zippers, and snaps.

I don't give a second thought that I'm sitting bare-ass naked in a captain's chair of a boat I've never captained before. I pull her down into my lap, onto my waiting cock.

Angelica hisses as I fill her, inch by inch, until she's fully seated precisely where she needs to be.

She's so wet and tight for me. Knowing I'm going to spill my seed into my wife, and that we're finally ready to create life from our love, makes the erection swell what feels like another three inches.

We remain still and calm at first, simply connecting before the storms in our loins take hold. Before the friction and the grinding and the urgency.

She's so perfect and sweet when she's on top of me, stroking my face like I'm her spoiled pet.

"What are you thinking about, Abel?"

I love the way she's in the moment. Every single second she's drinking in the sight, the smell, the sounds. I have so much to learn from her.

"I'm thinking about how I'm gonna have to flip you over and start plowing; I'm fucking dying."

She arches an eyebrow. "I was going to say, I was thinking how you're too pure for this world. But now I have my doubts."

With that, I make good on my promise to flip her over, but move us swiftly to the row of cushions along the bow. She's under me her hands gripping the rail, ass in the air, and my captain's hat on her head as I rut into her like a fucking animal in the wild.

"Abel. Abel," she chants my name with every thrust.

"Angelica, my good girl. My princess."

She looks back at me, still whimpering my name.

My words entwine around hers, and together we make

a song. A raunchy song with a heavy, pronounced beat with every push and pull.

With my hand reaching around her front, my fingers find their favorite spot, nudging her clit, working it in circles in tandem with our increasing frenzy.

Her eyes widen, then her irises roll back in her head and she smiles savagely. Hardly the innocent princess everyone knows and admires. She's my dirty girl, with a cunt that pulls me in and wrecks me every day.

We can go below deck and use the bed for slow, savoring lovemaking later. Right now, we're fucking.

I don't enjoy being away from her for even a second, but that's life. But whenever we come back together, the way we ravage each other is beyond words.

Angelica shatters around me as I explode into her, shouting and cursing. Such a lack of decorum for a princess, I tease her.

Moments later, we're raiding the galley before we begin round two. "What's next on the agenda, captain?"

I like that word in her mouth.

"Jacuzzi? Bed? Back to the bridge?" I offer.

She chews thoughtfully and swallows.

"We could go down to the laz and do it on the unicorn float."

I twist my lips, thinking about all those floating toys. "I'll have to get out the pump and inflate it first."

Angelica's foot drags up my leg. "But, honey, I love watching my deckie pump his toy for me."

My wife's dirty mouth makes my cock twitch back to life all over again.

My teeth grit. Angelica arches a brow, her approving gaze on my cock. "Better get going."

"Aye aye, captain," I say.

What the princess wants, the princess gets.

. . .

THE END

THANK YOU FOR READING SHIPPED! *If you enjoyed this story, please consider leaving a review wherever you prefer to buy your e-books.*

Please visit my website at authorabby-knox.com for information on lots more titles to read. While you're there, be sure to sign up to receive my newsletter to keep up with my latest releases!

About the Author

Abby Knox writes feel-good, high-heat romance that she herself would want to read. Readers have described her stories as quirky, sexy, adorable, and hilarious. All of that adds up to Abby's overall goal in life: to be kind and to have fun!

Abby's favorite tropes include: Forced proximity, opposites attract, grumpy/sunshine, age gap, boss/employee, fated mates/insta-love, and more. Abby is heavily influenced by Buffy the Vampire Slayer, Gilmore Girls, and LOST. But don't worry, she won't ever make you suffer like Luke & Lorelai.

If any or all of that connects with you, then you came to the right place.

9 798223 527947